Listen to the Leaves

Stories by
Lisamarie Lamb, Yagni Payal,
Cathy Graham, Ajo Despuig,
Ann Partridge, Teodora Savu, Jamie
DeBree, Mary Fleming & Carol R. Ward

Listen to the Leaves
ISBN 978-1-937477-54-7
Copyright © 2012 Brazen Snake Books
All rights reserved.

Edited by Jamie DeBree & Carol R. Ward

Table of Contents

Landscapes
by Lisamarie Lamb

Aiden shuffled through the leaves lying on the ground. He loved nothing more than to crunch the crispness under his feet, the air frigid and visible around his head.

He loved these woods too. They were Aiden's playground – he always preferred natural climbing frames, real adventure, to the colourful monstrosities that the council liked to install in the middle of housing estates, or on the edges of perfectly fine parks. The older boys liked to hang out in the one near his house where they smoked and drank and talked about things that scared little Aiden.

Things like girls.

So he went to the woods.

Aiden waded through mud in the winter, picked at the green shoots in the spring, hid from the sun in the summer, and kicked through the leaves in the autumn. On his own. Always alone. Which is exactly what he wanted.

Until the day he found her, the lady. He named her Julie. When Aiden first saw her, she was lying on a log in the middle of a deep pile of leaves, her eyes closed, her coat discarded and left to hang over a grey tree branch, her scarf wrapped tightly around her neck and her hand dangling down, barely touching the ground.

He stopped. He made no sound, not wanting to wake the woman. Girl. She was young, though older than him. A teenager maybe, but not much more.

Aiden watched for a while as the woods became darker and the birds became quieter. The girl didn't move. She looked so peaceful that Aiden didn't want to disturb her, so he crept away and when he was far enough down the path he broke into an excited run, desperate to tell someone about the girl.

Because she had been beautiful.

Before seeing her, Aiden had never been interested in girls. They held no fascination for him like they did his schoolmates. Girls frightened him a little and they worried him a lot, and that was all he needed to know.

Julie was different.

Aiden couldn't quite put his new feelings into words. He couldn't quite understand what was happening, but he knew he had to see his girl again. He gave her a name so that he could talk to her at night, and he gave her a life so that he could practice what he would say to her next time they met.

He stayed away from the woods – from anywhere – for a week, just rehearsing what he would say, and imagining how she would respond. In his mind, she always responded well. She agreed to be his friend, to play with him in the woods, to hang around with him at home. Maybe one day she would even take him to the cinema, or buy him a burger.

Aiden smoothed back his hair and dressed in stiffly ironed jeans and a striped shirt that was supposed to be saved for best, for church, for visiting. It was not meant for wandering in the woods, and certainly not for clambering over fallen trees and splashing through leaves. Aiden knew he would catch hot hell from his parents when he returned home that night, but for now he was happy. Off he went into the woods to find Julie. And he did find her. Exactly where he had left her the week before.

Julie hadn't moved. Her clothes fit looser now, her coat was covered in a layer of light moss, her fingers, dipping down low into the leaves, were blue tinged and pale. As Aiden drew closer – closer than he had before – he saw that they had been nibbled at by some small creature with big teeth.

It didn't occur to him that this might be a bad thing. He understood that she was different. Strange. He felt then that she was a lot like him, so he didn't mind. The smell was a little off-putting, but she did live in the woods. What did he expect, really? And clearly she was one with the woodland creatures.

Aiden couldn't – or wouldn't – see the truth. He sat next to Julie and chatted on and on. He talked more to her than he had to anyone else for as long as he could remember. He loved it.

He trotted home with a smile on his face, full of the news of his new friend. His new, quiet, tired friend.

He planned to tell his parents about her but when he arrived home he saw that the house was full of people. Some he knew and some he didn't. They brushed him aside and he sat and listened to them for want of anything better to do.

A girl was missing. She had been missing for just over a week, and it was time the locals did something. The police were taking too long.

A flier fluttered down to the ground and Aiden saw Julie's face. A fuller, pinker, happier face, but it was her nonetheless. The boy's heart broke, understanding too much all at once. His friend. His only and best friend. She was going to be taken from him, they would insist that she went home, and he would have no one to talk to.

Rather than waiting to comb the woods with the volunteers, Aiden slipped away. Out into the dark, into the trees and beyond to where Julie lay, yellow skinned under the moon's light.

His beloved leaves would keep her safe. He dragged her down to the ferny floor and knelt beside her, whispering his plans, his dreams, telling her not to be afraid, that he would look after her.

And then he piled the leaves on top of her body, and listened to her reply.

###

About the Author

Lisa loves to write horror, but dabbles in various genres, including mystery and children's stories. She has written and published a horror novel (*Mother's Helper*) and a collection of short stories (*Some Body's At The Door*), and has recently completed her second novel (*At Peace With All Things*).

Her work can be found online at http://www.themoonlitdoor.blogspot.com, and within many anthologies including books from Angelic Knight Press, Cruentus Libri Press, and Sirens Call Publications.

She has also edited a collection of short stories (*A Roof Over Their Heads*) set on and around the Isle of Sheppey, Kent (UK) where she lives.

Ruby
by Yagni Payal

June 6th, 2006. It was the happiest day of my life. Her one 'yes' after a million 'maybes'.

Today, entangled in wedlock, this quantum paradox sticks out like coarse grey hair. Forsaken, the raped sky mocks the prickly void inside, in realistic optical illusions. I climb the Penrose stairs every day, within her illusive torturing chambers as a hypnotized lover, tunneling back and forth, traversing through her pores, her follicles, her pale flesh and skin, flash correcting and fixing bent frames of us, together.

I am still here.

I hear faint baby wails as I cock up my left ear and eyebrow. The dog whimpers. Hell, I am still here!

That flicked cigarette butt discarded still burns. (It has been lifetimes). Flipping over and over again as it finally comes crashing head-on, colliding against my being in holes. We were at the beach making love, laughing, chasing gulls and counting stars. The waves were lit. That ill-fated night, why did I let her drive alone? If only...

There is no God.

My tottering beliefs sag like double chins, quivering in regrets and with trembling cold hands I cup the smoke and quickly pocket it along with her throbbing memories. Her soft breasts, the smell of her hibiscus shampoo, the way her long lashes drew beautiful mosaic shadows over her chiseled nose, the way she kissed with her eyes open and ran her long delicate fingers through my hair, stirring mayhem, the chilling haunt of moments.

One by one.

And the *Man* in the backstage cheers and whistles. Lunatic. Why does he keep following?

As an epic black yawn engulfs the sleepless night, it's dawn, it's dusk, it's dusk, it's dawn. Slowly as concentrated lifetimes go by, my wrinkles settle in, comfortable between hair and chins and arms. The *Man* smiles, sometimes his irises dilate and change color to reflect her glowing face. I cannot watch, my chest tightens and I find myself pouring another strong drink. The countless bottles and mountains of ash portray the residual proof of a growing habit and a living, burning corpse.

Every passing minute, I wait for the clicks. I wait for the tocks. It has been an endless count. I waited 6 years for her to finish her PHD in Psychology. On her 29th birthday, I gifted her a revered Dali'ish automaton clock and waited patiently for her to say 'yes'. But I was last on her singing bucket list.

And the *Man* loads up his red pick-up truck with flowering cacti, as if he is erecting a tall gravestone. A dangling blue shoe, from when I was two, sways in the wind's ABC song, taunting from the dashboard. I lost my mother then. That was the first time I had seen the *Man*, bending over her body and inspecting it inside out like a shaman. My drunken father had handed me an ABC cube to distract. I felt nothing then. I played. Now the swinging shoes with tattered black laces prick like needles inside my brain, defiant and alive.

Outside, falling dry leaves form patterns of her name again and again in fluid motions. *Gemma*, I miss you. But the blackbird has been long buried. Deep inside the cuckoo clock, long dead. Our wedding song floats in and carries with it her Degas ballerina silhouette dotted with red flowers that never got a chance to bloom.

Hey Man! Do you hear me? Should we play a part in this together? Should we take her apart? Unwind? Rewind? Resurrect her?

And glue it all back? The wrinkled yellow leaves, all her rusted pink parts? Pump her nostrils? Heave her chest? Mend her wings?

One by one.

And place them back on the punished fallen trees, leap frogging between quantum deaths and finite breaths? Tossed by overbooked tornado workshops of twisted fate and emotional turmoil, life's whirling flowers stalking like shadows behind painted finger nails? Like nothing ever happened, reset?

And the *Man* in the camouflage shirt swiftly sweeps, humming our favorite love-song "*Brushstrokes in the sky, only YOU can finish that painting. If I am the start, you are the end*". My blind carpet of denial thickens and spreads virulent in sync with his rapidly increasing grin.

He laughs as if reading my mind, mocking its pain. Dark exhaust fumes from his accelerating red truck propel a tumbleweed of crunchy leaves, to rise and snake within the patterns of the grey scarf she wore that night. Now, her flickering epitaph reads "*She dreams, she sleeps*".

But it's not her grave. Not Gemma's. It's mine, buried under her cascading hair and her horizontal spine.

The slow afternoon burns, smelling of charred maple syrup. A flightless baby cuckoo appears once and burrows itself further deep, in hushed slumbers, paralyzing time's numbing pendulum swings.

One by one. Like nothing ever happened. Like nothing ever will.

The red truck fades, the fumes behind it chasing like ghosts. I light up another useless cigarette. It glows red like my ruby eyeballs. The license plate screams "He dreams, he weeps".

###

About the Author

Yagni is a multi-faceted creative artist. She has been writing poetry since her very early years. Her poems have appeared in USA's The Copperfield Review, Danse Macabre, Quiet Magazine, Vox Poetica and UK's Forward Poetry. A playwright, actor and director, also a wife and mother to two beautiful children, Yagni resides in southern California.

The Treehouse
by Cathy Graham

Tory stretched out on the log and let out a long sigh.

"You worry way too much, girl," Tory's friend Celeste said, blowing a cloud of cigarette smoke into the clear forest air. "You need to live in the moment like I do."

Tory's long brown hair splayed out against the log and she closed her eyes wishing she was alone. This was her special place to think and Celeste was ruining it for her. Clutching a handful of dried leaves, she crushed them between her fingers. She sat up, adjusting her favourite grey scarf that her childhood friend Dan had given to her years ago. The weather was getting colder, giving her a good excuse to wear it more often. Shaking her hair out over the scarf, she looked at Celeste in her fur coat and heels.

"Is that what you call living in the moment? Just look at the way you're dressed. When I invited you to

the farm, I thought you might dress more appropri-
ately."

"I'm a city girl. I don't fit into this country life like
you do, Tor," Celeste said, crushing her cigarette butt
into the dirt.

"Why did you agree to come with me then?" Tory
asked as they walked along the path. Celeste kept trip-
ping on roots and Tory had to reach out to steady
her.

"I wanted a change of scenery. I haven't been out
of the city in months. You're not still mad at me
about Norm, are you? It was only one kiss, honest.
We were drinking. You know that."

Tory had been trying to put Celeste's latest stunt
out of her mind.

"I'm trying to forgive you. I really am," Tory said,
her lips in tight line. The image of Celeste and Norm
embracing flashed in her mind. "Actually you did me
a favour. I wasn't that into Norm anyhow."

When Celeste had offered her the waitressing job
and let her stay at her apartment, Tory thought it
would only be temporary. Three years later she was
stuck in the same situation. So much for her dream to
have her own cake decorating business and become
independent.

"Hey, look!" Tory said, pointing up. "It's still
there."

They looked up at the remnants of the tree house Dan had built when they were kids. Tory and Dan used to spend hours up there.

Tory had made a birthday cake for Dan's seventeenth birthday, but had dropped it on the way up the ladder. It had fallen to the ground breaking into gooey chunks but they still ate some of it, even full of ants, leaves and dirt.

The woods came alive with the sound of rustling leaves and thumping paws as a Golden Lab ran up to greet them.

"Hi there, sweetie," Tory said to the dog as she scratched its velvety ears. Celeste cringed and kept her distance.

"You know I don't like dogs. Keep it away from me," she said, her nose wrinkling.

"Bailey, come here, girl!" a voice called. Tory felt her heart race as she saw Dan coming towards them.

Dan looked at Tory for a long time without saying anything. "Good to see you, Tory," he said, his face guarded. "I heard you were back for a visit."

"Good to see you, too. Gran said she invited you to Thanksgiving dinner tonight," Tory said, trying not to show her eagerness. Dan looked the same and smelled the same too, the pungent aroma of manure clinging to his boots. Dark shadows smudged below his eyes and a few lines etched the corners of his mouth. His curly brown hair was shorter than he used to wear it but he was still basically the same Dan she had known since she was a kid.

Celeste cleared her throat to remind them that she was there. As if anyone could forget Celeste.

"Hi! I'm Celeste and you are gorgeous!" she said. Celeste gave Dan one of her cougar looks as if she was ready to eat him up.

Tory glared at Celeste but she ignored her.

Celeste stumbled along the path and grabbed Dan's arm for support. He helped steady her and pulled away, his face reddening. Tory wanted to slap her as she was taking her femme fatale act a bit far, but she was always that way where men were concerned.

The autumn leaves rustled as Bailey ran through the forest to retrieve the ball that Dan threw for her. There was a definite smell of winter in the air that made Tory shiver. At least she thought that was what was making her shiver. Every time she looked at Dan, she wanted to say something but her mind had gone completely blank. Dan, too, was lost in thought while Celeste chattered enough for the three of them.

They came to the end of the path where the forest opened up to the street.

"So are you coming back to the house with us?" Celeste asked, putting her hand on Dan's arm.

"I'll be there after I finish the milking," Dan said, gently pulling out of her grip.

"See you later, Handsome!" Celeste said with a wink.

"Later, ladies. The cows are calling," Dan said, looking relieved to escape.

Tory watched him go, an intense longing washing over her at seeing him again. How could a man look that gorgeous in a stained baseball cap, dirty overalls and manure-caked boots?

Hadn't she always been ashamed of being a farm girl and of the whole farming community? Hadn't she left home when she was seventeen, determined to never come back?

"Do you think I scared our poor farmer away?" Celeste joked on their walk back to the house. "Isn't he scrumptious, Tor? I'd let him plough my field anytime." She licked her crimson lips. "So, is Dan an old flame? Tell me everything."

"We were just friends." Tory said, not wanting to tell Celeste about the huge fight that had hastened Tory's departure.

"I don't believe it," Celeste said. "Men can't be just friends. It's always sexual. You guys had something going. I could see it in the way he looked at you."

"He's a good friend. That's it." Tory felt heat rushing to her cheeks.

"If you're not interested in Farmer Dan, I'd love to put my shoes under his bed." Celeste winked at Tory.

"Celeste, the heels are so high on your shoes they wouldn't fit," Tory said. "Besides, he's twenty-seven and you're thirty-nine. You're much older." Unease pricked at her. She didn't want Celeste going after Dan. He was way too good for her. She'd eat him up and spit him out. But Tory didn't want him for herself, did she? Being a farm wife was the last thing she wanted, wasn't it? She had always fought against being stuck out here in the country. Confused thoughts ricocheted through her brain.

"So what? Lots of older women go for younger men. If the chemistry is right, why not? Besides, I only want to have a little fun with him. I'm not the marrying kind, unless they're rich," Celeste said, hobbling along the road like an old lady in her heels. She stopped to light another cigarette and blew a cloud of smoke into the air.

"You smoke too much," Tory said, coughing. "You're too much, period."

"I know. All the guys say the same thing," Celeste said with a laugh as if it was a compliment.

"Well, about time you two got back," Gran remarked when they finally walked into the kitchen. She was standing at the sink peeling potatoes. "I've got lots of jobs for you girls to do."

Tory groaned. So much for her relaxing weekend.

"I want you to be kind to Dan," Gran said, tossing the potato peelings into the compost bin. "It's hard for him since his divorce came through."

Tory saw Celeste's face light up at the mention of Dan's name. That look always meant trouble.

"Divorced you say? Aw, the poor baby. I'll make sure to give him extra attention. Gee, I'd better hurry and get ready." Celeste rushed to her room.

"Your friend is quite the piece of work, isn't she?" Gran remarked once Celeste had gone. "Do you think she's a good influence on you?"

"What do you mean?" Tory said, bristling for another of Gran's endless lectures.

"I hate seeing a woman like you with so much potential throwing her life away."

"Who said I'm doing that?"

"Being a waitress and hanging out with Celeste at bars is not my idea of how to realize one's potential."

"What do you suggest I do?" Tory finally said in frustration.

"What ever happened with your dream to have a cake business? You were always so good at that. You're so creative."

Tory took a deep breath and pinched her lips together so that she wouldn't scream. "Okay then. Why don't I make a cake for dessert?" She rummaged in the kitchen to find all the ingredients and cake pans.

Putting on an apron, she got to work and found she was enjoying herself. She couldn't remember the last time she had made a cake.

Gran knocked on the bathroom door and cornered Celeste who was putting on makeup in front of the mirror.

"Okay, that's enough primping. I need someone to do the vacuuming," Gran said, pointing to the vacuum cleaner. Tory stifled a giggle at Celeste's look of confusion at being asked to help out. Reluctantly, she took the vacuum and started cleaning.

Tory took a shower and changed into a vibrant green wool dress that showed her curves nicely. She even applied makeup, something she rarely did. Why did she feel she was competing with Celeste?

When Dan showed up, Tory rushed to the door so Celeste wouldn't jump his bones the minute he arrived. Poor guy had been through enough.

"Hi," he said with one of his slow grins that had always made her melt. "You look fantastic."

"Hi," Tory replied, her mouth dry. "You look great, too." He wore an Irish knit sweater and brown corduroys. He looked so good it took her breath away. For once he didn't smell like manure. His spicy cologne made her want to snuggle closer.

Dan reached out and tweaked one of her strands of hair. "I'm glad you didn't cut your hair. I've always liked it long."

"Dan, I really need to talk to you about something," Tory began but Celeste pushed past her.

"Hi Dan," Celeste gushed. She put her hand possessively on his arm.

"Hi Celeste," Dan said with a nervous smile. He stood there like a petrified mouse about to be pounced on by a hungry cat.

"Don't make the poor boy freeze. Invite him in," Gran shouted from the kitchen. Tory took Dan's coat while Celeste led him to the living room and made him sit on the couch beside her. Why was Celeste doing this? Didn't she know she was driving Tory crazy?

The aroma of roast turkey filled the air and mixed with the smell of Tory's cake.

Gran had decorated the dining room with a fancy red tablecloth, an autumn leaves centerpiece and her best china. There were even candles burning in Gran's brass candle holders. She never got those out unless it was a special occasion.

"Sit beside me, Dan," Celeste urged, patting the chair next to her.

"Quit telling him what to do, Celeste," Tory said, gritting her teeth. "Let him sit where he wants."

"My goodness! What's wrong with you?" Celeste said, her heavily made-up eyes widening in surprise. "Is it that time of month?"

Dan sat next to Tory, an expression of relief on his face.

"So how are things, Dan?" Gran asked, carving the turkey while Tory passed the mashed potatoes.

"Can't complain," Dan said as he took a drumstick from the tray that Gran offered him. "No one would listen anyhow. Wonderful dinner. Thanks for inviting me."

"Wait until you see the surprise Tory made for dessert," Gran said, beaming with pride. "You remember how good she was at baking. And she's so artistic. I always say it's a shame she didn't become a professional cake decorator."

"I still remember the beautiful birthday cake she made me for my seventeenth birthday. It fell out of the tree house and broke but we still ate it and it was good, too," Dan said.

"What a cute story," Celeste said in a fake voice that made Tory want to puke.

Gran and Tory cleared the dishes while Celeste chattered to Dan.

"Celeste, we could use some help here," Tory said. "I have to get the cake and coffee."

"But I'll ruin my nails washing dishes," Celeste complained, waving her long red nails about like cat claws.,

"I have rubber gloves," Gran said and threw her a pair. "How do you ever work as a waitress with silly nails like those?"

"Today was a special occasion," Celeste said, winking at Dan.

"Can I help with the dishes?" Dan offered getting up.

"Of course not. You're our guest," Gran said.

"I thought I was a guest, too," Celeste grumbled under her breath as she gathered dishes.

Tory brought the decorated cake from the kitchen and placed it on the table.

and brought it to the table.

"Well, would you look at that?" Dan said with a delighted laugh. "It's the oak tree with our tree house in it. I love it. Hope you got a picture."

"Nice cake," Celeste said leaning over to take a closer look at the round layer cake adorned with a carefully drawn oak tree. At that moment, she dropped the plates she was carrying and the cake was flattened, all the decorations smooshed together.

"You wrecked my cake!" Tory cried.

"It's these nails. I'm so sorry," Celeste apologized.

"You must be some waitress," Dan said, shaking his head.

"I'm so tired of your games, Celeste. You think life is one big party. Well, I'm sick of it!" Tory said, fuming with anger.

"Big deal, it's only a dumb cake," Celeste said with a shrug. "I'm sorry. What else do you want me to do?"

"You're acting like a flirt throwing yourself at Dan. It's driving me crazy."

at the two women fighting over him.

"What's your problem? You said he was just a friend," Celeste said and her eyes widened. "You've got a thing for Dan. I knew it all along."

Tory's face flushed and Dan looked at her in surprise.

Celeste took out her cell phone and checked the messages. "I think I'd better go now. Sorry you're sore at me, Tor. Call me when you calm down." She put on her fur coat and grabbed her tote bag. "Thanks for the great dinner."

The door slammed with a loud bang. "Good riddance," Tory said.

"Wow, is she for real?" was all Dan could say, shaking his head.

"Why I'm friends with her is beyond me," Tory said. She returned to the dining room, and looked at the squished cake in dismay.

Dan took a broken chunk of cake and bit into it. "It sure tastes good. And there's no grass or dirt in it either, just turkey gravy. Here try some." He put a piece of squished cake in her mouth. Tory giggled. The giggle turned into a hearty laugh. She took a piece of cake and pushed it into Dan's mouth. They smeared each others face with cake and icing, exploding into fits of laughter.

"What's so funny?" Gran said coming into the room.

"Nothing," Tory said and they laughed harder.

Gran just rolled her eyes and sighed, a smile tugging at her lips.

Tory looked out the window at the snow falling.

"Let's wash up and go outside."

They quickly cleaned up and got their coats and boots on. They walked along looking up at the slow snowflakes swirling through the air like moths around the streetlight. Tory stuck out her tongue and enjoyed the sensation of the cold snow melting in her mouth.

"What a beautiful night. I want to walk in the forest," Tory grabbed Dan's hand with eagerness and pulled him along.

"But it's so dark in the woods,," Dan said.

"That's why I have this," Tory said, shining her flashlight under her chin so that the light cast harsh shadows on her face.

"You look like a witch," Dan said laughing.

"Mwhwahaha! Not as bad as Celeste. Now there's a witch if there ever was one," Tory said.

"That woman is incredible. Hard to believe she's for real," Dan agreed."Where did you ever meet her?"

"At a bar. I wish I could just erase her from my mind," Tory said. "Or better yet, from my life."

"Then why don't you?" Dan said, serious all of a sudden. "You don't need someone like her dragging you down."

"I was grateful for her help when I was at a low point in my life. Now I think I've outgrown her."

They walked through the forest enjoying the silence of the woods as the falling snow deadened the sound of the crunching leaves.

Dan turned to look at her in the glow of the flash light. He stretched out his arm and touched her grey scarf. "Are you still wearing this? I gave that to you ages ago. fallen apart by now."

"I love this scarf. I've kept it for years to remind me of you," Tory said, glad he couldn't see her face reddening. She cleared her throat gone dry again. "I'm sorry about how I treated you years ago, Dan. I was young and stupid."

"It's okay. I know you didn't want to be stuck out here. You wanted to see the world. I get it."

"I've seen some of the world. I went out West and traveled around. I enjoyed it for a while but it wasn't that great. Now I know what's important."

"Yeah, what's that?" Dan asked.

"Family. A sense of roots," Tory said and paused. "And good friends like you." She squeezed Dan's hand.

"You can change your circumstances, you know," Dan said.

"You're right. I'm still young. I can travel. Have a new career. And we're still friends, right?"

"Of course. I should never have asked you to get engaged when we were only seventeen. We were just kids. What did we know? And I know you only thought of us as friends anyhow."

"I lied about that." Tory ran ahead, thoughts jingling in her head like loose change.

Dan rushed to catch up and grabbed the end of her scarf.

"Not so fast. You can't say something like that and run away. So tell me how you really feel."

Tory hesitated, her heart pounding.

"Out with it," Dan urged, pulling her into his arms.

"I'm crazy about you," She rested her head against his shoulder. "Always have been right from when we were kids. But I've been horrible to you. I wouldn't blame you if you hated me now."

"I was mad at you," Dan said. "It hurt to be rejected." He rested his chin against her hair. "But hate you? That could never happen. You make me feel whole in a way no other woman could." He leaned down and kissed her. They embraced for a long time in the darkness. Falling snow melted on them but they barely noticed.

"So does the offer still stand?" Tory asked looking up at him in the dim light of the flashlight.

"I don't know what you mean," Dan said in a teasing tone. Tory could tell he was enjoying making her uncomfortable.

"Are you going to make me grovel and beg?" Tory said.

"Yes, I love to make a woman beg," Dan joked. "I have that effect on females, especially my cows."

They walked hand in hand, arriving at the big oak tree with the tree house. It was now or never. She made Dan sit down on the log.

Tory got down on a bended knee in the snow. "Dan, will you please marry me?"

"Yes, I certainly will," Dan said, pulling her onto his lap. "But only , but on one condition"

"Name it," Tory said, leaning her head against his chest.

"You quit waitressing and do your cake business," Dan said. "I'm ordering another cake, by the way. That's two you owe me now."

"Sure thing, boss," Tory said. "And we can have Celeste be my maid of honour."

"Maid of dishonor is more like it," Dan joked.

"No way I'm inviting her. I didn't like the way she looked ready to devour you like a female praying mantis. Made me so jealous."

"I'm glad she came for Thanksgiving dinner," Dan said.

"You are? Why?"

"Because she forced you to confront your feelings and make choices about your future. She is good for something after all." He removed Tory's scarf and re-arranged it around her neck. Grabbing the two ends, he pulled her towards him and gave her another kiss.

"Just think. You'll be my husband. Love the sound of that," Tory said, stroking his cheek. She held on tight as if she was afraid she might be dreaming. "And I already know what I'll call my baking biz."

"What?"

"Piece of Cake."

"You and your awful puns," Dan said, groaning.

"You should talk," Tory said, pulling his hat down over his eyes. "Naming your farm 'Milking it for all its worth' is pretty lame, too,"

"Face it. We belong together," Dan said, taking one end of Tory's scarf and wrapping it around his neck until the two of them were hopelessly intertwined.

###

About the Author

Cathy Graham is happiest when she can be creative whether it be writing, playing flute, singing in a women's choir or doing photography and scrapbooking.

Cathy has had short stories published online and in print as well as a children's Christmas play. She especially enjoys romance and children's writing. She lives near Ottawa, Ontario with her husband, two teenage sons, two dogs and two cats.

Autumn
by Ajo Despuig

The air is filled with the sober scent of autumn as I cross the street on my way to the park. I walk rather hastily because the coffee that I purchased a few minutes earlier is starting to burn the skin of my hand. I switch my hold on it from time to time to escape the mild smoldering sensation.

This is my favorite time of the day, a time wherein I can be with myself. Spending eight hours pushing papers and beating deadlines can be lonesome. My young wife will not mind if I take an hour or two at the park, sipping brew and reading a book. She gave me the book anyway.

I have the afternoon all figured out in my mind. After my brief sojourn, I'll go back to my office parking lot and grab my bike then paddle my way home. I might stop by a good pizza place three blocks away from my apartment. I will eat dinner with my wife, play with my young son, watch the daily news and then prepare for bed.

Then I remember- I have a pending report due tomorrow morning at my supervisor's desk. I guess I'll just finish this coffee and go back to the office to accomplish it. Goodbye paperback, pizza dinner and family time.

The park is serene as usual and the only creature stirring aside from myself is a squirrel on the ground chewing on something but fled after seeing me. The brown autumn soul is all around and the grass is laden with a mass of dead leaves. I notice that my coffee is cooling. There is a bench and I walk towards it.

I sit down and I realize how tired I am. I glance around the brown scenery and see a girl laying on the dead mass of brown leaves a few steps away. I wonder what is wrong with her. Should I check? I stand and move towards her before answering the query. I leave my messenger bag and the book my wife gave me but I still hold fast to my cup of coffee.

I walk slowly through the leaves so I will not stir her. The late afternoon breeze blows from behind me and moves the brown mass towards her. That's when she notices me. A smile forms from her lips. The girl is pretty. Her black hair is sprawled along the grass. She is wearing a red turtleneck and a grey ombre scarf which blends well with the autumn scene.

"Is that coffee for me?"

"I drank a few sips it all ready but you can have it if you want."

"I was just kidding."

I do not know how to carry on the conversation.

"Are you just gonna stand there or will you keep me company?"

I smile at her in reply.

"It is a wonderful afternoon ain't it? Do you come here often?"

I know I have to answer. "I usually come here if I have time. Enjoy a cup of coffee and read."

"Do you like books?"

"I do."

"Me too. I like the classics. What about you?"

"Any book will do for me. The book I have at the bench over there which was given to me by my wife."

She looks at me blankly. I see her left wrist is covered in bandages.

"Lie beside me," she said.

"Why?"

"Because it is a good day for lying on dead grass and for listening to the hymns of the leaves."

"You are poetic."

"Oh, only when I am lying on dead grass."

We both laugh.

"Come and listen."

I kneel beside her and I realize how beautiful she is but I cannot take my eyes off those bandages. She notices my curiosity.

"I sometimes cut myself so I might feel alive. Pain does that, you know. Reminds that you are alive. Some people need to make money to feel alive and there are some who need to cuddle with a partner or a mistress. I feel alive and important. Every movement that I make, every shift to the left or right, every crunch makes me feel important. Try it."

I set the half- finished coffee down but I knock it over as I lay down. I feel the crunch of leaves and the crack of twigs. I am still worried about her cuts when the spilled coffee touches and burns my hand.

About the Author

Ajo Despuig is a Filipino writer residing in Quezon City, Philippines. He graduated from the Far Eastern University in Manila with a degree in Literature. He likes writing poetry and short fictions. He does not like coffee but loves lying down on dead leaves with girls.

Listen to the Leaves
by Ann Partridge

I've tried to be the mother I wish I'd had.

My children are young adults making their way in the world. All three of them are good people. None of them are geniuses or anything approaching international celebrities. None of them are drug addicts or in prison for other unlawful activities. On the whole, I'm satisfied.

I hear from them regularly. Not every day, but mostly every week. I can tell how they're doing by how often they call me. If I hear from them more than once a week, it means they are having trying times and need a mother's opinion, or more often a mother's ear. If I don't hear from them during a week, it means they're doing great and I don't have to worry.

Right now, they're fine and I'm a little lost.

Yes, I know that I am more than just a mother. I'm also a wife. Pat and I have been married almost thirty years. We have our moments, but there are more good ones than bad. I'm a receptionist at a local doctors' office. I'm an animal lover, though the last of our pets - Malarky, an Irish setter, had to be put down last month.

I'm also a daughter, though my father has been distant since he married Cynthia and moved to Cleveland. My sister and I refer to her as "Cyn," though in our minds she is "Sin." She is just what you would expect from the neighbor who took advantage of our family's bereavement and moved into our home within a month of our mother's disappearance.

I was eleven years old when my mother vanished. That was over forty years ago. My younger sister Nancy was eight and our little brother Robert was just six.

The whole ordeal left Dad broken. He had been a confident, warm man whose ringing laughter brightened every corner of our little house. Afterward he never lost his bewildered look of loss. Years of talking to police, private detectives, newspapers and making public appeals had turned up no signs of his wife and our mother. Suspicion had fallen on him and the police and media had pried into every minute detail of our lives. None of Mother's things were missing and there was no evidence that she had formed any kind of relationship outside our home.

There was no evidence of foul play, but no way to prove that it hadn't happened.

Most neighbors avoided us as if we harboured a contagious condition except Cynthia, who insinuated herself into our family by taking over household chores that we were too numb to undertake. She gradually took over the duties of wife and mother until she was a necessary, if often unwelcome, cog in our family machinery.

At school, I remember the sudden silences when I would enter a classroom. Teachers tried to treat me normally, but the pity in their eyes hardened my resolve to keep my feelings to myself. I never wrote about the ordeal or mentioned it at school. By the time I reached high school, I was accustomed to being whispered about. Teenagers gossiped about everyone, so I didn't feel particularly singled out anymore.

Nancy and Robert were younger and wore their loss openly. Despite my attempts to pretend everything was normal and to encourage my siblings to accept the situation, they appeared needy. I thought we should change our last name to Lost. The Lost family.

After a dozen years with no new information, the courts declared Mom legally dead and after we three children had left home, Dad married Cynthia and moved to a place where no one recognizes him as the man who misplaced his wife. I sometimes wonder if he felt he owed her marriage, for her years of devotion to our wounded family.

My sister Nancy and I still occasionally speculate on what could have happened to Mom. We consider odd scenarios like alien abduction or the witness protection program. Maybe she witnessed a mob hit on her way home from the grocery store. I know, I know … I said they were odd. We refrain from mentioning anything truly horrific like abduction and murder or willful abandonment. Our brother Rob refuses to talk about Mom at all. He calls Cyn his mother and leaves it at that.

At loose ends, I'm meeting my sister Nancy this afternoon to look into a mystery at a local retirement residence where her daughter is employed. My niece Serena finished her Personal Support Worker program and started working at Sunshine Acres (cheesy name, I know) in the nearby town of Port Welcome. Serena is my sister Nancy's oldest daughter, but many people say she resembles me. While Serena was at work, an elderly woman suffering from Alzheimer's addressed her as Maureen. More than once. I just realized you might not understand the significance of this. I'm not sure if I mentioned that my name is Maureen Gordon. It is, and so this elderly woman mistook my niece for me or it could be just a coincidence. Serena says this woman has days when she is quite lucid and other days when she is not.

After relaying this information to me, my sister Nancy posed the long unanswered question, "Could it be Mom?'

Through the years members of our family had dutifully offered to be interviewed when contacted by the media on anniversaries of Mom's disappearance. The stories ran every five or ten years but never convinced anyone to offer any new information, so it seemed unlikely that our mother could have been within hailing distance and not tried to allay our anguish.

"Is it possible she's been living only 35 miles from us all these years and we have never known?" Nancy asked me.

"I can't imagine how, but let's go together and investigate... unless ...you don't want to. We don't have to. Is not like it really matters now...it won't change..."

"Of course it matters, Mo," Nancy interrupted my stammering. "All these years of wondering what happened. Serena says her name is Ann Kelly."

"Ann is not far off Angeline, but I don't know where the Kelly could have come from unless she remarried. That would be bigamy. Maybe she just took that name. Maybe she lived farther away and just ended up in Port Welcome when she needed medical care."

"Will you recognize her, Mo? You were older than me and have more memories. We have photos, too."

"I'm sure I will, if it is her. Let's go and find out…more likely the whole thing is just a weird coincidence."

I tried to convince myself that it was purely an academic exercise at this point in my life. After all it's not like I was still the stunned girl whose mother vanished one day never to be seen or heard from again. I'm a happily married mother of three and soon to be a grandmother. Did I mention that before? My oldest daughter Patricia is expecting her first child just before Christmas. I'm excited about it, but also a little nervous, because it will once again challenge my view of who I am. Once I'm Grandma, there's no going back to the old younger Maureen, is there? I didn't express that well, but you can catch my drift.

Okay, maybe it's not just an academic exercise, I think later as I fight the urge to throttle the white-haired old lady who is prattling on about gardening. The eyes are the key. The hazel green outlined with gold. They aren't as clear as they used to be, and the intelligence doesn't shine through any longer, but the resemblance to my daughter Patsy's eyes is unmistakable. I hadn't realized I had memorized the shape of my mother's fingernails and hands and the way they tapered at the wrist.

Nancy was gripping my hand hard and silent tears were streaming from her eyes. I steeled myself to not give in to emotion. It wasn't like it was a reunion. This old woman, who definitely was our mother, didn't show any sign of recognizing either one of us.

I wanted answers and not about which plants preferred shade. What the hell did, "Listen to the leaves," mean, anyway? I wanted to shout, "Where the hell have you been? Why did you leave?" I could feel myself shaking with suppressed rage.

We went to talk to the retirement residence administrator after realizing that our mother, who wasn't aware she was our mother, was not going to offer any useful information today.

Nancy's eyes, swollen from crying, were of more use than my clipped tones in persuading the woman in charge to talk to us. Looking at Ann Kelly's file, she revealed that she had no family, no next of kin listed and the only information of any use was that she had been living at Sunshine Acres for three years and prior to that lived in a rural residence 10 minutes outside of town. We got the address from her and decided to canvass any neighbors to see if we could find out how long she had lived there, or who with, or anything. We made an appointment to talk to the facility's doctor the next day.

When we found where our mother had been living we were appalled. The name Kelly was on the rusted mailbox, but it appeared to be an abandoned cabin all alone at the end of a gravel road. There were no neighbors to talk to. The roof was at a decided slant and the front door hung agape at an angle. Both front windows had been smashed. The climbing red roses beside the front door offered the only colour.

We walked through the deserted building and apart from frayed curtains that reminded me of ones in our childhood kitchen, Nancy and I saw nothing of a personal nature. Nature was moving back into the cabin and there were signs of wildlife inhabiting the space. The mold and mildew sent us back outside soon in search of fresh air.

There was a maple woods on three sides of the house, I noticed. If Mother had been listening to the sound of the wind in the leaves, there was a lot to hear. If the phrase was significant, I failed to see how. I wondered if perhaps there was more than Alzheimer's wrong with our mother. Maybe she had always been slightly off centre, though I had no memories indicating that.

I was burning now with the need for information. I wondered if Mother had papers or documents stored at Sunshine Acres.

"So who are we going to share this amazing story with?" I ask Nancy after we partially process the shock.

"Dad and Rob?" she says.

"They would try to grill her and it would only add to her confusion," I offer.

"Serena?" Nancy suggests.

"She can keep her ears and eyes open for developments," I agree.

"What about a private investigator?" Nancy asks. "I don't think either of us can afford it," I admit. "Unless you know someone who knows someone...?"

"Not that I can think of. So what else can we do?" she says.

"All I can think of is to take turns visiting Sunshine Acres and hope one of us is

there on the day she is able to tell us her story."

I didn't know how long I could stand to be patient. You would think it wouldn't matter to me anymore, but I'm burning with the need to know who or what pulled our mother out of our lives. I can actually feel my face and body burning. Okay, it could be a hot flash, but I feel like jumping up and down and screaming at the top of my lungs. I guess it wouldn't be fitting for soon-to-be-Grandma Maureen to take a temper tantrum like a toddler, but the idea appeals to me.

Okay, so we've been visiting "Ma Kelly" for a couple of weeks. She has never once referred to me as Maureen, though she has occasionally repeated the process with my niece Serena. I guess Serena is closer to the age I was when Mom vanished. My mother never knew me as a teenager, or in any of the decades since. Sad…for both of us, I guess. Other than repeating "listen to the leaves," the old lady hasn't revealed anything of note. It seems the talk about plants and trees is what happens on her lucid days. She doesn't want to discuss people or places. Apparently she was a fine gardener and if I was so inclined I could learn what to grow where. I consider the idea and then disregard it. If I was going to have a green thumb, it would have been apparent before now. I'm over fifty for God's sake.

I'm worried that the visits are taking a toll on Nancy. She seems prone to tears and wants to reminisce endlessly about our childhood. Until now we had buried most memories from before the disappearance and I find it painful to dig them up again. If her expression is any indication, she does too. We are at an impasse. I wonder if the government would have any record, tax returns, etc., of Ann Kelly and if those records commenced after Angeline Green's ended. I'm burning with curiosity. Or hot flashes. Anyway I'm on fire.

On one of my days at Sunshine Acres, I tell Serena that the wondering is wearing me out and I need to figure out how to investigate Ann Kelly's history. I'm hoping that she knows about some popular web site or app that lets you trace someone's history. Yes, I've Googled it, but haven't discovered anything satisfactory unless you count court divorce papers that cite Bruce Springsteen, which can hardly be applicable.

Serena doesn't know about a magic web site or app, but she does have someone she went to school with who is attempting to get into investigative reporting and offers to give her a call. I agree, because I don't have a better idea. The notion that Mother had her paperwork stored at the retirement residence has proven to be unfounded and I don't know what government agency I can contact that won't alert the authorities and thus the rest of our family. Mom's physician doesn't have any medical history that pertains to her mental condition other than her Alzheimer's that is evident at every painful visit.

Serena's friend Rache (for some reason she leaves off the "l") loves the idea of looking into the story, takes down what little information we have and goes off to investigate. In the meantime, my children seem to be doing well without me, and I am becoming obsessed with the mystery of my mother. I've started wandering around the abandoned Kelly place on the days that I visit "messed-up mother." I have a crazy idea that Ann Kelly had buried her paperwork during her gardening forays. I have even examined the grounds to determine what kinds of plants she was trying to grow as if they would provide clues as to why she was there and not with her husband and children.

These outdoor investigations prove fruitless. I'm no closer to discovering the whys of my abandonment than I was before the abandoner was located. I seem to be permanently burning. The only things I do find at the Kelly place are a series of trails through the maple woods. Walking them becomes part of my thrice-weekly routine – painful Sunshine Acres visit, drive to the abandoned Kelly hovel, walk the trails through the maple woods. I listen to the wind in the leaves, but it has nothing to say.

On one of these walks it occurs to me that I miss Malarky. I need to have a companion to walk these trails through the woods. Before I can weigh this decision, I stop at the Humane Society on the way home. Without consulting my husband, I sign papers and adopt a Golden Retriever mix. Pat is surprised when I come home with a rambunctious canine. He (Pat, I mean) opens his mouth to protest, takes a look at the high colour in my face and pets the dog.

"What's its name?" Pat asks.

"Flash," I answer while I'm having one.

"Ah, Flash Gordon," Pat comments.

I don't laugh. I do, however, roll my eyes, while thinking that it is a good thing I gave that name to the dog before my husband started using it as my nickname.

Pat also tells me Richard called. Richard is our youngest child. It's been over a week since I've heard from him, so I figure he is good. Pat knows nothing to indicate otherwise. Rache calls to set up a meeting with Nancy and me. I'm impatient and want her to disclose all she knows on the phone.

Trolling through the County land registry, Rache has discovered that the property where Mother had been living never belonged to her. She must have been renting that old cabin. The property owners for over 70 years were a family named Beech. They had once lived locally, but somewhere through the years the heir to the property had moved out of the area and the township had been unable to say where. The taxes were paid annually from a trust set up with a lawyer in Port Welcome. He wouldn't divulge any other information.

That didn't get us any further ahead as far as I could tell. Without being able to talk to the landlord we wouldn't be able to find out how long Mother had been hiding out in that old cabin. Surely she hadn't lived there for forty years.

Rache had tried the post office, to see if they could tell her how long they had delivered mail to Ann Kelly at that address. She had been hoping for someone who had worked the rural route for years and would offer the information freely, but as it turned out postal information is protected by a privacy act and not available without official documentation. The hydro at the cabin was also paid for out of the trust with the lawyer and he wouldn't say anything one way or another. The cabin had been heated with a wood stove, so there was no record of Ann Kelly signing up with oil or gas companies. There was no record of a phone at that address.

Rache had been thorough with the little information we had given her. She had gone to the library and read the newspaper stories written at the time Mom disappeared. She suggested we get the police to reopen the cold case as they would have access to government records regarding Ann Kelly aka Angeline Stevenson. She must have filed income tax or registered for a pension, driver's licence or some other official document. The government would have her address on file and we could at least see where she had been living and when. It might even be possible to see when she assumed that identity or if she ever filed taxes jointly with anyone else. It still wouldn't tell us why, but it might be a beginning.

After the meeting with Rache I took Nancy and Flash to the maple woods around the former Kelly cabin to walk the trails and discuss what we should do. We figured if the landlords weren't local, there was little chance they would worry about people using their woods. Flash walked very well on his leash and only tried to dislocate my arm once when a squirrel crossed our path.

Nancy and I wondered if our mother had walked these trails. We thought it very likely. Maybe she had even made them. Had she had a canine companion to coax her out in all weather? We were constantly coming up with new questions. Should we go to the police and tell them our mother, who was after all officially dead, wasn't? What would they do? We had tried talking to her and hadn't had any success. What would her reaction to uniformed officers be? Would they understand that she wasn't withholding information deliberately? Would they notify the media and were we up to dealing with all that again? It would mean telling Rob and Dad and Cyn, who had managed to put all this behind them.

Perhaps members of the public would recognize Ann Kelly and offer snapshots of her life. Were there worse things to worry about than your mother disappearing? Had she founded a suicide cult? Was she on the run for murder? Or something worse? We couldn't think what that would be, but we did wonder if it was a Pandora's Box kind of deal, going to the police. The biggest question was whether we would be doing it for selfish reasons such as raging curiosity at the expense of the old lady's peace of mind. Not to mention that of our other family members.

The shady maple paths worked their magic. Nancy and I decided to play it by ear. We were going to make a more concerted effort to talk to our Mother without scaring her with demanding questions. We were going to do it together for a while and see if we could ferret out any tiny tidbits of information and only inform the authorities if we thought they wouldn't do her harm. Yes, we were burning with curiosity, me more than my sister, but it wasn't actually vital that we know now. Because after all, what would change? Only the story we tell ourselves about who we are.

A week or so later Nancy and I were visiting Ann Kelly, aka Mom. We had patiently heard the diatribe on preparing the soil to grow perennials. When the topic seemed to come to a natural end I said to Nancy in an offhand manner, "The leaves are starting to fall. The reds and yellows are giving way to browns. I think they are telling us that another season is coming to an end." Yeah, I know it sounds lame, but I was looking for a way to demonstrate that I was listening to the leaves.

Wide-eyed, Nancy followed my lead. "The rustling sound when we walk on the maple trails makes me think I could almost understand a message."

"Listen to the leaves," our mother said, yet again.

"What message did the leaves give you Ann?" I asked nonchalantly.

"It was a warning," she said while deadheading her red geraniums.

"That winter was coming?" I asked at a loss.

"An end of life indicator," she said.

I was thrilled we seemed to be having a normal conversation, though I was still having trouble following it. Nancy and I looked at each other with raised eyebrows. I guess winter could be considered the end of life for many growing things. Staring at our mugs on the tray, I had a new idea.

"Who was reading the leaves, Ann?"

"Geneva," she answered.

"Geneva Acorn," Nancy said.

Our mother nodded affirmation as I looked at Nancy with raised eyebrows once more. We'd moved from leaves to nuts without a smooth transition as far as I was concerned. Nuts in both definitions of the word.

"She used to have a little storefront on Birchmount," Nancy explained. "Tarot cards and tea leaves read on Thursday evenings and Saturday afternoons. We dared each other to do it when we were teenagers. Only Chrystal ever went. She was thrilled, though."

That kind of rang a bell. A midnight blue doorway with stars and moons suspended over the window. A psychic had given Mom a warning. Was that what all the "listen to the leaves" talk was about? "What was the warning, Ann?" I asked. If we referred to her as Mom, she refused to talk to us.

"The end of…" Ann suddenly looked at me in obvious confusion and stopped talking. She looked at Nancy next and then went to her rocking chair in the corner and started rocking rhythmically and humming loudly.

Having experienced similar behaviour on other visits Nancy and I got up and bade her goodbye for now. She didn't acknowledge us again. We walked out

of Sunshine Acres wondering how to find out if
Geneva Acorn was still alive and if it was possible she
could remember Mom's reading in light of the fact
that Mom had disappeared. That was the first glimmer of information we had received, though even if
we found the psychic I can't imagine she could shed
any light on Mom's disappearance. It did, however,
demonstrate that some of what Mom said made a
weird kind of sense.

Just days later Rache called to let us know she had
located Geneva Acorn and got us an appointment to
meet her at her son's home in Davenport. She was
over ninety, had limited sight and mobility, but still
had her wits about her. Kind of the opposite of Mom.
We were impressed that Rache managed to find her
and a little abashed when she said she went through
local telephone listings for Acorns and called them.
Apparently Acorn is not a common name. Why we
didn't think of it, I'm not sure. Maybe because it was
so simple.

Geneva's grey-haired daughter-in-law brought us
tea after seating us in a cozy sitting room with her
mother-in-law. The tiny old lady looked like a child
sitting in a grown up's chair. Her thinning hair was
snow white and she wore thick-lensed glasses that re-
flected the light back at us. She was wrapped in a rain-
bow-striped crocheted afghan and used both hands to
steady the tea cup that was placed in her hands. Once
we were sure she could manage her beverage, Nancy

and I sat back on the sofa and sipped our tea. I let
Nancy explain the reason for our visit and the faint
hope that this miniscule woman would remember
Mom's reading. When I heard Nancy say it out loud,
it sounded like we were maybe demented ourselves.
Geneva listened intently, but didn't look in our direction. She was still for so long, that I wondered if she
had nodded off.

Finally she nodded and said in a remarkably
strong voice, "I remember."

I almost wore my tea. Nancy gave a gasp of surprise. I was looking at the woman with a pleading expression that she likely couldn't see as I waited for her
to say more.

"Warned woman her life was almost end. Days
only. Evil one take it."

I was biting my tongue to keep from interrupting.
Nancy gripped my hand as we waited for more to the
pronouncement. When Geneva didn't say anything
else, I looked at Nancy and tried to breathe evenly. I
wanted to ask the right question and not pepper the
little seer with all my scatterbrained inquiries. I had
just decided what to ask when Nancy commented,
"The woman didn't die, though."

"Lost life," Geneva said, nodding her head in affirmation.

"She lost her life with us," I said to Nancy quietly.
I turned back towards Geneva and asked, "Do you
know who the evil one was?"

The small psychic with the big voice continued to nod, almost rocking. Finally she said, "Leaves no say. Please to finish tea"

Crushed with disappointment and burning with questions, I gulped down the now tepid beverage until I started to gag on the tea leaves. Geneva could either see better than I gave her credit for or she recognized the gagging sound because she held out her hand. I was confused whether to shake her hand goodbye or help her up until she said, "Cup."

I handed it to her and she lifted it up to her eyes and peered into it while holding it level. Then she reached her hand in and felt the leaves. She started nodding again. The suspense was doing me in. Finally I asked, "What do you see?"

"Leaves," she said.

No shit Sherlock, I thought. I could feel myself heating up. I didn't see how this meeting was going to end in anything other than frustration.

"Leaves show leaves. Evil one not close. Not gone. Spark help," Geneva pronounced. She held her hand towards Nancy who dutifully handed over her cup.

Following the same ritual which seemed to take forever, Geneva finally said, "Women walk leaves. Three. Days only."

Following this cryptic information, she leaned back in her chair and closed her eyes. She waved her hand in a gesture that could only be interpreted as dismissal.

Nancy stood reluctantly and I followed her lead. As we made our way to the doorway, I called out, "How could the evil one take her life?"

Geneva shook her head slowly and then said, "Look to see."

On the drive home Nancy and I debated possible meanings for the psychic's confusing words. There weren't many of them, but they still sparked weird questions. Did *evil one* mean the devil? Did *not close* mean he was in hell? *Women walk leaves* – what on a leash? *Three* what? Three women? Three days? How could the evil one take a life without murder? *Spark help*? Would the evil one spark help? That made no sense. *Look to see*. Now, that was just the sort of re-mark one would expect from a crystal ball charlatan. I was feeling despondent. The only concrete thing to come out of the visit was a confirmation that our mother did have the odd nugget of information in her head. Did we have patience to dig out more, though?

Next morning Nancy calls me early sounding ex-cited. "Mo, could we take Mom for an outing?"

"What outing? Why? When?" I asked. I wasn't yet finished my first cup of coffee and I'm not at my best early in the day. My husband and children know not to try to talk to me until I've had two cups.

"I've been thinking about what Geneva Acorn said. Women walk leaves. Three. It makes sense if you and me and Mom walk the trails in the maple woods. Three women walk in the leaves. Mom might find it familiar and it might spark some recollection in her mind. Remember Geneva mentioned a spark, too?"

"Hmmm," I muttered unconvinced.

"It would be worth a try. You could bring Flash because he'll need a walk anyways. It might be better than sitting in Mom's room trying to get her attention."

"Hmmm," I offered again.

"I'll call Sunshine Acres and see if they'll let us take her out today. Because the other thing I got thinking about that Geneva said was "days only". She said it in her warning to Mom and she said it again about women walk leaves, so I thought we should get right on it."

"Right," I agreed. I wasn't sure if I agreed with Nancy's interpretation of the psychic's words, but it was something else we could try.

I had worried that Mom would be reluctant to get in and out of the car or be afraid of Flash, but those fears were unfounded. What happened was that she seemed to be nervous about walking outside. She held her arms out far from her side as if she were balancing on a tightrope. Finally, Nancy and I took pity on her and each held onto one of her arms to keep her feeling secure. After that she walked along quite well, though she offered nothing in the way of conversation. We couldn't tell if she felt comfortable in the woods, recognized the paths, or wished she weren't there. She didn't put up any resistance coming or going and didn't give the abandoned cabin a second glance. So, no new revelations, but a better activity than sitting in Mom's room, so we decided to repeat the experience in two days when I had another day off work.

This time the sun was shining and it was a gorgeous fall day. Just a hint of crispness in the air and the gold and red colour of the maple leaves was almost neon bright. The sunlight caught Flash's golden coat and he seemed to fit in perfectly on the woodland path. As the three of us were walking, Nancy and I each holding one of Mom's arms, I remarked, "Nancy who would have ever thought we could spend part of such a perfect day going for a walk with our mother in this beautiful maple woods?"

"We didn't even think we had a mother," Nancy commented.

I nodded and reached over and squeezed Mom's shoulder. She looked at me curiously and then over at Nancy. I wondered what disjointed thoughts were running through her mind. Did she recognize where she was and who she was with? I thought not. It was still a great day for a walk.

Then something darted across the path and Flash's sudden lunge jerked the leash out of my hand. "Sorry, Mom," I said, "I'll be back in a flash with Flash." I left her with Nancy and ran ahead to where Flash had treed a squirrel and was barking at the base of a tree. Above him, high up in the branches the squirrel was chattering down at the dog. It seemed as if he was telling Flash off for chasing him. I laughed and tugged the reluctant dog back the way we had come.

When I spied Mom and Nancy, Nancy looked excited. "Ann pointed out something in the bark of that tree," Nancy said and pointed.

When I walked over and examined it, I gasped. The initials A.S. were carved into the bark. Angeline Stevenson, our mother's real name. I looked over at Mom, who was looking around with every sign of recognizing where she was. Flash started digging at the base of the tree. I tugged on the leash until Mom said, "Dig. Dog dig."

"Mom?" I said tentatively and placed my hand on her shoulder.

She looked at me. There was no recognition. She had melted back into her morass of confusion.

"Listen Mo!" Nancy exclaimed.

Flash was still digging furiously, but we could hear his nails hitting something solid. I reined in his leash and pulled him away from the hole. I handed the leash to Nancy while I went back to discover the buried treasure. I tried using the toe of my shoe and then got down on my knees and using both hands I unearthed a tin. Rubbing the dirt off the surface, I could see it was one of the tins that people used to buy festive shortbreads in at Christmas. With a little tugging and cursing, I managed to open it. Inside was a crumpled brown paper bag. It was the size of a lunch bag. I unfolded it, but there was nothing inside it and nothing else in the box. I was about to toss it all away when I noticed handwriting covering the bag. It was handwriting I recognized from my report cards in early public school. My mother's writing.

"Nance, its Mom's writing!" I said. I started reading aloud, *"I, Angeline Stevenson, am here against my will. I could easily get away but if I do my children and husband will be harmed, in all likelihood murdered…"*

"Mo!" Nancy's shout stopped me. Mom had slipped to the ground.

"Mom, er Ann, what is it? What's wrong?" I asked.

She couldn't or wouldn't answer. I jammed the bag in my pocket and bent down to help Nancy get Mother back to her feet. She stood with the support of both of us, but we had to work to keep her upright. I wondered out loud if we could join hands and support her full weight between us and get her back to the car that way, but I didn't know what to do with Flash and his leash. I pulled the handle up as high on my arm as it would go and then Nancy and I carried our mother to the car. Flash seemed to know something was wrong. He didn't tug on his leash once, and stayed near us. We were as gentle as we could be, but I fear it was a rocky ride for Mom.

Flash leaned gently against her in the car. We took her back to Sunshine Acres because they have a nurse available and a doctor on call. The nurse seemed to think that Mom had just overdone it. All her vitals were good, so she just settled her in her bed and said she would call us if there was any change in her condition. When Mom was sleeping, Nancy and I went out to the car and read the rest of the story on the brown paper bag together.

"No one would ever guess the identity of my abductor or believe me if I told them. Though it's as simple as ABC, I have no proof to offer. There is nothing in writing or recorded. I have been left in this desolate spot and if my jailer returns at any time of the day or night and finds me not here, someone I love will come to harm. I believe the threat because of what I was told about her spouse's death. I can stand to live here, but what I can't stand is knowing that my family will think I have abandoned them. Even if I could somehow disable my captor and I was free to return to John and the children, they would not welcome me because they were made to think that I had deserted them. They would be hard pressed to believe that someone they know could be so ordinary on the outside and so evil at heart. I wish I could get word to them anonymously, but I'm afraid the truth could lead to their deaths. I don't know how long I can live in this isolation under a false name and

without my loved ones. Sometimes when I walk through the forest, I can hear my children's voices in the sound of the wind in the leaves."

"Jesus, Mo!" Nancy wailed. "When I think of all the terrible things I wanted to say to her …."

"I know, Nance. I know. I thought of every one of them and wanted to throttle her when I first laid eyes on her a couple of months ago. The poor woman probably lost her mind years ago. I don't think mine would stand up to that kind of torture. But, who was it? Who was the evil one? She said it's someone we know."

"I'm sure she said she."

We read back through the heartbreaking testament and found "her spouse's death."

My cell phone rang. It was Rache saying she had something to show us. I told her we had something to show her, too, and agreed to meet for coffee in an hour. My phone rang again. It was the nurse at Sunshine Acres saying Mother had taken a turn for the worse. Luckily we were still in the parking lot. Nancy and I raced inside.

Mother couldn't be woken. She didn't seem to be in any pain, but somehow she had slipped into a coma state. We sat with her for a while and felt guilty for the negative thoughts about her we had harboured for most of our lives. It felt like we were losing her just when she was returned to us.

Then I got mad! Nancy and I shouldn't feel guilty. Neither should Mother. All the bad feelings can be laid at the feet of the evil woman! I had a glimmer of insight just as my phone rang again. It was Rache wondering where we were. We explained Mother's health deterioration and asked if she could come to Mother's room. I didn't think this discussion would upset the unconscious woman.

When Rache arrived I quietly told her about our walk in the woods and the initials in the tree and Flash digging out the document that was worth more than any buried treasure to two formerly abandoned daughters. I gave Rache the paper bag to read and she handed me an old yearbook from the Port Welcome high school.

"Remember I told you that the Beech family owned the property that your mother's cabin was on? I've been trolling old newspapers on microfiche to see if I could find out anything about them. I struck out. But I noticed the library had old yearbooks going way back, so I've been working my way through the B's. I've gone through a few years and anyway, I finally found a Beech."

I turned to the page Rache had bookmarked in the yearbook. There was only one Beech. I recognized her. Speechless, I handed the book to Nancy.

"But she wasn't a Beech," Nancy said. "Her last name was Ash."

"Beech must have been her maiden name and Ash her married name. They're b-both leaves, you'll notice," I sputtered hysterically. I could feel rage building inside me. I felt like I could burst out of my skin like the Incredible Hulk.

"Cyn! God Damn, Cyn! We should have known. The evil one took Mom's life. She actually stole it for herself, but she didn't really get Mom's life because none of us were ever the same again. Look to see, Geneva Acorn said. Look to see!! The authorities will be called in now you betcha, baby. That Sinful woman can't pay enough for our loss of trust in the world! It was as simple as ABC – Ash, Beech, Cynthia! Dad is going to lose another wife, but at least this time he'll know why." I was shouting in the room of a comatose woman. I wasn't thinking straight.

Nancy was pale. In shock, maybe. Rache was crying after reading the paper bag message.

The machinery attached to Mom started to sound a loud alarm. She was leaving us again.

Nancy and I leaned over the bed as the nurse indicated the time had come. "Listen to the leaves, Mom," Nancy whispered. "We know your truth now and you are free to leave to a less painful place."

I added, "We know that you were on an involuntary leave of absence, Mom, and you'll be in our hearts as long as the leaves dance in the wind."

I'm sad to lose my mother so soon after I found her again, though she was never entirely with us this time. It's like she stayed long enough for her story to be discovered. I feel bad for our brother Rob losing the woman he considers his mother. Nancy and I will try to help him through it.

I guess I'll never be as strong and selfless as the mother I found again and I can't imagine being anything like as evil as the wicked stepmother I ended up with. On the whole, I'm satisfied. I think, before I call the authorities, I'll call my children and share my story and some of theirs.

About the Author

Ann Partridge is a member of Northumberland Scribes, a writers' group in Cobourg, Ontario, Canada, which helps motivate her to sit at her computer and put thoughts into words. She has had pieces published in two Rattles Flash Fiction anthologies and has completed her second Nano – which means she has over 100,000 words towards a novel. Ann is a compulsive reader and enjoys making and sipping wine.

No Autumn Changes
by Teodora Savu

"It's a beautiful autumn day... and I am a monster."

Autumn is the season that brings changes. All kinds of changes, the most interesting and the most frightful you can think about. Trees begin to change colors, the temperatures become cooler and you are made to put your shorts and your sleeveless shirts away. You bring out your warm sweaters and your jacket, you stuff your flip flops in a cupboard and take out your boots. When the leaves begin to change colors, the people change their usual activities. Some of them, those who have been going to the beach and to try to steal the sun from the sky all summer long go back to work or school. The others, on the other hand, they start going for drives and trips to the mountains, needing to enjoy that mystical place all by themselves.

But are all the changes autumn brings so nice? What are we talking about? Silly, optimistic thoughts we think will make us feel better, while the flat world keeps going the same way. The shades of orange, yellow and brown replacing the live electric green, the trees stretching their branches for the last time before having to meet the cold breeze, all bare and naked. The Moon keeping her big eye on the Earth, while the sun gets to sleep in. What change do they make in this dull world? The guy who goes on a trip to the mountains, playing his music, drawing his love, moving away from all the other people and retiring in a world of his own... How does this form of unsociability help him solve the problems he has?

That's what he thinks about as he walks the empty alleys of the park. And that's what he has been thinking about for the past hundred years. He reads a lot and he sees what people's opinions are on seasons, rain and other natural phenomenons. They think their life is changing, they think these are those hidden agents that give them new thoughts and ideas. Such cliches, such a silly perception on what real life is... . Autumn, instead of causing him all those stereotypical sensations, has always caused him the contrary. Everyone wishes for a fairytale world for himself, an idyllic, naive, hyperbolized world where he can hide, away from the real world. Why hide from it? Why not accept it the way it is, rough and hard?

He has never understood the concept. But maybe this is just because he is not a normal person anymore. He is not a person anymore, actually, nor a human being. Maybe these thoughts are right for people and he doesn't get them just because he is so different from them. He looks around the park as he stuffs his hands in his pockets, protecting them from the cold wind. His blonde locks fall down in his eyes and on the back of his head, while his porcelain skin meets the anger of the frozen air and the furious clouds.

Autumn is a season of desperate hopes. The leaves are souls begging to turn life on pause. Begging to stop, begging to take a break, hiding under smiles and childish words. As they break off the branches, they start changing in the wind; for the worse in the eyes of silly people, but for better in his eyes. Souls, leaves are photographs of a beautiful life. They live it so shyly and innocently, not making a difference between the good and the bad because they do not live long enough to learn and to understand life's constant battle. They fear the wind and they fear the change; it's in their nature.

What was in his nature? He was the opposite. He was the one that made them understand how all this was, what life was and that they didn't have to be afraid of the wind, because he was the wind. A leaf may die in a matter of minutes, hours, or maybe even days after it meets the wind, but during that time, it lives the time of its life. It learns and finds out so much, things about what it actually is, then dies happily, not caring that it was nothing in this world and that the great ones have just crushed it without even noticing. This is what he does. No one can tell him that he is mean, bad, or the king of the dark. He feeds on souls, but this doesn't mean that he doesn't have a soul of his own. He is not the bad guy, not ever. He is a kind teacher, willing to share his wisdom with others... in exchange for their lives.

At some point in this second life of his, he got bored and felt that he needed a comrade to help him get through eternity. Eternity, the end of the world – these all have turned into such common notions, exactly because no one knows what they are. But when you meet with your fate and you realize that you are going to live until the end of the world, you feel like running away at first, because only then do you realize what it means and how much it takes.

He picked Cosme after he studied three people for one month. One of them was an army veteran who now talked to young soldiers and made them understand that the possibility of dying in war didn't have to be stronger than their love and their patriotism. The second one was a middle-aged man who had lost his wife and daughter in a car accident he had caused. He became self-destructive, cynical, spent his life drinking and taking drugs. He longed for the release of death, but lacked the courage to put an end to his days. And then, there was Cosme. The successful young man who, having finished studies, was working to become a neurosurgeon in one of the best hospitals in the country. The one who thought that his work and his occasional flings were the most important part of this world, the one who put himself in front of anything and anyone. And the one who was afraid of death... he was afraid of the wind.

That made the man choose him and none of the others; that made him want to teach him the reality of life and make him understand what real value was. After turning him into one just like himself, he realized that Cosme was scared. He was not as bold and brave as he had thought at first and the change was overwhelming him. It was that change that led to despair and fear.

'Why?' he kept asking, breathing too quickly and moving too fast.

'Because that's who I am,' the man would reply simply, fixing him with his stormy grey eyes.

'This is not who you are,' Cosme tried to convince him. 'You are good person, Kalev.'

But Kalev would just shake his head and walk out of the room. 'You don't know me at all, Cosme...'

This discussion happened this morning, before the blonde-haired, porcelain-skinned, human-looking creature left for the park. He walks now, chuckling to himself and shaking his head. He is a good person, sure... . What does Cosme know about this anyway? He is just a kid. He is twenty-five years old and can look mature among his family and friends, but he is just a kid making his first steps in life.

As millions of thoughts flood his mind and his whole body, he accidentally bumps into someone. The person's notebook falls on the ground, and he gets down to pick it up. He does so and gets back up, hands the object to the woman and looks straight at her. His ice blue eyes seem to be looking right into her soul. Funny how in this situation, that expression is actually a real verbiage of the truth.

"I'm sorry..." he speaks lowly, a tiny smile creeping on his lips. The brown eyes and the dark hair, they seem to be those of a female version of Cosme.

"Not a problem, I was not paying attention," she smiled shyly, her cheeks color changing into a soft shade of pink. "I'm Cornelia," she says, and holds out her hand.

"I'm Kalev," he nods slightly as he shakes her hand. An electrical current runs through her whole body under the frozen touch as his gorgeous eyes seem to be burning holes into her brain and her heart.

"So, are you the rocker type?" she smiles, trying to cover her obvious feelings and sensations. She points at the leather jacket and the little skull drawn on his shoulder as she speaks. Her voice is dull and she is not very pretty, but he feels like she would make an interesting prey, a good student; not a follower or a comrade.

"I would rather describe myself as someone interested in life, and especially death," he says.

His voice is chaotic and hollow, a tiny part of a dark, unknown world. A shiver runs down her spine, but she can't move away. She is so captivated that she can't take any step further from him.

"You do?" she asks softly, losing herself in his now greyish eyes. "Interesting. It wouldn't work for me though. You may call me a chicken, but I am kind of scared of all this."

And there she is, telling him exactly what he wants to hear. "You are scared of death?" he asks, slowly passing his tongue over his teeth. She stares at him blankly, seemingly hypnotized.

"Yes..." is all she can say at this moment.

The corners of his lips curl up into a smirk as he gently takes her warm hand and strokes her tanned skin with his thumb. "Let me take this fear away then."

Only minutes later, his red lips are only centimeters away from the dead girl's pale ones. Her dark hair is falling back, allowing him to see her plain face. His blonde locks are touching her soft cheek and her chin as he, like the marble statue of an extravagant artist, steals her soul, like he had stolen so many others.

"What are you doing?" he hears a faint voice in the distance.

His blurry, sleepy eyes raise from the girl's face and look up into a pair of dark brown eyes. "Feeding..." he mumbles, his lips not even moving.

"I really thought you were a good person," the same voice says.

Kalev rolls his eyes and swallows a bit. He drops the body as if it was just another object, and slowly advances towards the other man. He wipes the corner of his mouth with the cuff of his jacket and runs a hand through his messy yellow hair. His long fingers trace a line against the young man's cheek and jawline as he looks him in the eye.

"It's still a beautiful autumn day, Cosme... and I am still a monster," he shrugs indifferently, then starts walking away.

About the Author

Teodora was born in Constanta, Romania, but when she was three years old, her family moved to a small town not far away. She has always liked to write, especially essays and short stories. As for reading, she likes fantastic literature, mystery and detective novels, but she is not that fond of romance.

She likes travelling and watching and playing sports, probably her biggest passion. She has taken TaeKwonDo classes, but she also loves tennis, badminton and soccer.

Lullaby
by Jamie DeBree

You're breathing too loud. They'll hear you.

The woman stopped behind a thick tree, her back to the trunk. She leaned over to brace her hands on her knees and drew in a long breath, letting it out slowly only to repeat the process. There wasn't much time. Even if they couldn't hear her breathing, they had to be getting close.

Run! Now!

With one last deep breath and a quick glance in all directions, she sprinted forward with no particular destination in mind.

Away. Must stay away.

It was impossible to move quietly through the colorful fall leaves. They crunched and floated around her feet as she ran, cheerfully calling out to her pursuers. The wind was her only hope, sifting almost constantly through the thick canopy above to direct an orchestra of sound and light that absorbed the cacophony underfoot.

It had been three weeks since they'd taken her. Twenty-one marks on a cold dirt cellar wall, fighting off rats of various sizes. She hadn't been able to beat them all.

Embrace the pain.

Her wounds throbbed against too-tight clothes borrowed from a stash she'd found hidden behind old crates. Another one taken, perhaps. A woman unlikely to be found, unless she'd somehow escaped.

Her foot caught on something and a searing sharp heat sent her sprawling. She lay there for a moment, closing her eyes, breathing, listening to the rattle and shake that filled the air. Maybe she'd just stay. Maybe this was far enough. Maybe they wouldn't--

Get up. Run. Survive.

She sighed. Pushed herself off the ground. Tested her ankle and winced, but took a step forward.

Voices. Run!

Stumbling forward, she moved, slower now. Her vision blurred, and fingers through her hair came back sticky. Had she fallen against a rock? A branch? Squinting in the dim afternoon haze she limped forward, tree to tree. The whispers seemed louder, and yet farther away. Somewhere a dog barked. Still she pressed on.

There were five of them, but only three were able to give chase - she'd made sure of that. She wasn't sure if the other two were alive or not. No matter.

They deserved to die after what they'd done. Animals, all of them.

Her belly clenched and she doubled over, falling to her knees. The drugs were powerful, but she was stronger. Bracing herself, she rode out the wave that rolled through her body, welcoming the chance to purge her system. Her throat burned even as her head cleared. After, she borrowed a not-yet-crunchy leaf to wipe her mouth before rising to her feet.

This way. Quickly.

She turned, confused by a voice not her own. It wasn't one she recognized - friend or foe. Trusting was folly, but she had little choice. It was direction in a reckless game.

Hobbling as fast as she could, she followed. Straight then right then left then straight, until she stumbled into a dry creek bed. The noise of the forest quieted.

Spotting a section of thick brush, she pushed inside, emerging into a small opening surrounded on all sides by the tall bushes. A heavy log had fallen through and she let out a grateful sigh as she went to it and sat down. She twisted and turned, checking all angles for an obvious way in or out of the alcove, but it seemed that through the bushes was the only option.

Rest.

Laying down, she peered up into the multicolor canopy and watched the kaleidoscope of color as it shimmered and danced on the breeze. So peaceful. Whispers rattled through the leaves like a lullaby, rocking her to sleep ever so gently.

Her eyes drifted shut, the trees singing to her even as flashes of her abuse threatened at the edges of her consciousness. The men, if one could call them that, had been gentle at least, though the drugs made her sick every time. She placed a hand on the small swell of her abdomen, repulsively curious. Not that it mattered. She'd do whatever it took to ensure their plan failed, though she suspected the inbreeding had already taken care of that. A face came to mind unbidden, a too-high forehead, sunken eye sockets, rotting teeth and a jutting jaw line moving over her while Mother looked on.

The smell of fresh raw earth mixed with the scent of unwashed bodies and cheap cologne, her head trying to believe it was over while her senses refused to let her forget.

She opened her eyes, blinking back tears while the leaves still danced merrily above. Was she ruined then? Was she doomed to live in that mental space forever? To remember whenever she closed her eyes?

No. There had to be another way. She sat up, one leg on either side of her perch. Her left foot found the ground, but her right swung free and she looked to that side. Hidden between the hedge and her log was a black fissure a couple feet wide and several feet long, as if a giant arrow had hit the earth and broken the skin.

Leaning over, she peered into the darkness. Kicked a rock at the edge into the opening. Waited to hear it hit bottom.

Nothing.

The leaves were singing again. She looked up, listening, swaying with the breeze. It was calm, peaceful. For a single content moment, she relaxed. Forgot.

Slipped.

###

About the Author

A full-time webmistress by day, Jamie DeBree writes steamy, action-packed romantic suspense late into the night. Her goal is to create the perfect blend of sensual attraction, emotional tension and fast-paced adventure, similar to the television crime dramas she's hopelessly addicted to.

Born in Billings Montana, she resides there with her husband and two over-sized lap dogs. She reads in a wide variety of genres including romance, erotica, action/adventure, thriller, horror and literary fiction.

For information on upcoming books, visit JamieDeBree.com.

Old Joe
by Mary Fleming

'*Fall*' *what a gloriously dull word*, thought CJ, who loved all words, even the dull ones. But *'autumn', now that word really conjures up all the 'seasons of mists and mellow fruitfulness' and here I am laying on my back, daydreaming and looking up into a canopy of gorgeous maple leaves, not quite red and gold yet but definitely past the fresh, bright green of summer. Maturing? Ripening? No, just getting older, past their prime - like me.*

Poor CJ was depressed and not without good reason. She was now all of twenty-three years old and had no job - her future a huge question mark. It caused her no end of worry. It seemed that everyone she knew was working, earning money, fulfilling dreams, getting on with life. Where did it all go wrong? Where did it all slide into futility for her? Four years of university and now what? She looked up and wondered if the leaves had the answer. Perhaps if she lay here long enough they would talk to her.

One of the favourite questions asked by various visiting aunties was, 'and what do you want to be when you grow up, CJ?' She had thought about that a lot. In fact, the question was still right there, un-answered, twenty-three years later. Oh, they still asked but omitted the 'grow up' part. In their eyes, at least she had achieved that much.

A shout brought her out of her dream world and back to the present.

"CJ, what are you doing lying there? Are you sleeping? We really need you down here, right now."

It was her sister, the good daughter, the one who was always there who kept or tried, in her case, to keep them all in line.

CJ groaned. *Oh no, not another round of that damned apple game or I start walking into the woods and just keep walking. I wonder how far I would get. Would I meet our resident bear and what about that family of foxes? Would my family miss me? Would anyone?*

They all told her she was just a teensy bit difficult to live with, and sometimes, well she had to agree. Oh yes, you bet they would miss her; she was the only one who could come up with the correct answers to any and all of the dumb games they played.

Ha, I am good for something after all

If there were any prizes like cookies or candies riding on the outcome of the latest goofy game then they would realize how important she was to them.

"CJ, are you deaf or something? Get down here; we really, really need you, right now!"

Sighing, she got off the bench and made her way back down to the cottage. Quite a crowd had gathered. What was happening? She recognized some of the neighbours from other area cottages but wow, two police officers; they were not usually invited to the cocktail hour. The taller of the pair, and obviously the boss, was speaking and gesturing in all directions. He seemed to have taken charge of the group. What was he saying? She edged closer so that she could hear.

Oh! It seemed that the cute little curly haired boy from down the lake was missing and they were organizing search parties. Poor little fellow - he must be so scared.

CJ really liked him. She even talked to him, mostly about the trees. They were friends.

Oh, I hope he's all right. There are bears around and I wouldn't want anything bad happening to him.

She looked up into the leaves remembering their conversation just that morning. Suddenly, she knew exactly where he was. Well, she was almost sure but better not to say anything yet in case she was wrong.

That would not go down well. She would check it out on her own first.

In front of her, the crowd was being organized into small groups with instructions on what to do if there were any sightings. CJ inched her way to the back and disappeared into the trees before anyone could attach her to a group. Once in the woods she ran easily up the path.

All those daily runs have really paid off, she thought.

She pictured little Andrew in her mind walking along here earlier, singing to himself or talking to the trees.

"The trees are my friends," he had told her once.

Strange, lovely little boy she thought. *A bit like myself.*

She remembered that a couple of nights ago there had been a huge thunderstorm. Nothing was quite as dramatic as a cottage storm coming in over the lake, great streaks of lightening flashing and loud booms of thunder sending all the kids under a blanket giggling in mock terror. Of course the lights always went out, which made it even scarier. One enormous crash told the family that 'Old Joe' had been struck and had most likely crashed to the forest floor.

Their favourite tree, Old Joe, had been around forever - certainly as long as she had been coming up to the lake. Even dad remembered it from his boyhood summers at the cottage.

She remembered Andrew had been very sad, telling her, "I've lost one of my best friends. I have to go say goodbye to 'Old Joe' today"

That is exactly where she found the little fellow. He was sitting on the downed tree, gently stroking the bark and singing.

Then it hit her, she knew what she wanted to do with her life. She would look after the trees; become a 'tree hugger' as her father called all ecologists. At least Andrew would be pleased with her decision.

Yes, she thought I'll be good at that. Decisions are not so hard to make after all.

Wow, this had turned out to be quite a day. She went over to the boy, gave him a hug and patted the tree tenderly. They said their goodbyes to 'Old Joe' and then hand in hand they walked back to where the relieved group met them with hugs and cheers. She was a hero.

"How did you know where to look for him?" asked Andrew's mother.

"Oh I just looked up and listened to the leaves," she said smiling knowingly at Andrew.

After all, the trees were their friends.

###

About the Author

Mary Fleming is a member of Northumberland Scribes. She has lived in Cobourg, on Lake Ontario for the past fifteen years, but was born in Glasgow and is a passionate Scot This comes through in her writing where she very often slips into the local vernacular. She has written all her life but mostly for he own enjoyment never realizing that other people would be interested in her scribbles.

Message of the Ne'er Pan

by Carol R. Ward

They say only the desperate seek out the Ne'er Pan. The not-quite-sane. The abominations. For the Ne'er Pan is an unsainly place and ordinary folk would do well to avoid it. Listen to the leaves. They'll tell you so.

It was the time of the Aftermath, that which followed the Great Cataclysm of the Beforetime. Only rumours were to be had of the Beforetime and there were only frightened recollections of what caused the Cataclysm – the time when the very land itself was changed. Strange things were wrought in the Aftermath, not the least of which was the forest of Ne'er Pan.

In outward appearance it resembled any other forest; wild and green and teeming with life. But those few hunters who dared the Ne'er Pan reported no game to be found, no true forest noises save for the unnatural movement of the trees rustling without a breeze and eerie, muffled sounds that no one cared to put a name to. And there was also the mist,

that would appear out of nowhere and follow them like intruders.

On stormy nights, when the villagers huddled around their crackling fireplaces, tales were told of the Ne'er Pan. There was a pause every time a particularly strong gust of wind rattled a shutter, then the story would go on to tell of one brave soul who dared the forest's depths and returned a raving lunatic. Legend had it that the forest lived, and welcomed all that was unnatural.

You would never know to meet her that the girl was one of these unnatural things. She was one of the travellers, the folk who had no home. An herbalist by trade, she harboured a dark secret - a secret that would mean her life if it were ever to be discovered. Her success as an herb-wife was dependent on her healing touch, a touch that marked her as an abomination.

Her name was Ailiah - I overheard the villagers call her that. They often came within my hearing in their search for roots and herbs.

"Ailiah, come look at this herb, is it useful for anything?"

"Ailiah, I found some tubers for our supper."

"Are these mushrooms good for eating, Ailiah?"

Ailiah, Ailiah, Ailiah. It was a siren's song carried on the summer breeze. I would watch as she sang and laughed, the sunlight filtering through the leaves of the hardwoods to dapple on her face. Was I in love with her? Perhaps just a little.

I don't think Ailiah realized just how fanatic the villagers were when it came to abominations. They were one of the first to embrace the practice of burning them at the stake, though it never happened during her time in the village. But I remembered each and every one. Even from the distance I could hear the screams when it happened. And if the wind was in the right direction . . . the stench was horrifying.

The village had been without a healer for some time. The previous one had barely gotten away with her life - she'd been an empath, able to use her mind to find the root of someone's injury or illness. When she was discovered she escaped into the Ne'er Pan, and was never heard of again.

It is to be wondered that the villagers would trust another woman healer. But Ailiah was young and pretty, and won them over with her sweet disposition and her gentle touch. In a matter of weeks it was as though she'd always been a part of the village.

Her compassion was her downfall.

The village elder's young son fell down a crevice, near the edge of the Ne'er Pan, while playing a game of chase in the woods and broke his leg in three places. It could have been much worse. If the crevice had not been full of dead leaves from seasons past he could have split his skull open. I am not without feeling, had it been possible I would have ventured from my territory and attempted to heal him but fortunately Ailiah reached him quickly.

She climbed carefully down the crevice with sticks and cloth. This much I could see. The boy's mother insisted on climbing down with her, although I don't know what help she could have possibly been with all her weeping and wailing.

Sight was not needed to know when Ailiah straightened the boy's leg for splinting. He gave a piercing shriek that set a flock of grackles to wing and then was mercifully still. Whether it was compassion on her part, tiredness, or just plain absentmindedness, Ailiah let her control slip and sent healing energy into the boy. I may not have been able to see it, but I could feel it.

What the boy's mother saw only she could tell, but she didn't. Tell that is. At least not at that point.

Though I strained towards them to hear, I could only catch muted whispers, swift and violent. At last they called up to the others that they were going to carry the boy further along the crevice to where the walls were not so steep so as not to injure him further. From there they returned to the village and the incident was all but forgotten.

The days began to shorten and the leaves began to turn, their crisp contours much louder in the wind than summer's soft green. A troupe of roving entertainers made their way slowly along the edge of the Ne'er Pan, on their way to winter in one of the great cities to the east.

When the villagers discovered the troupe had sheltered in the Ne'er Pan for the night, they were both impressed and a little repulsed.

"How did you dare?" they asked. "How did you survive?"

"How is it you have lived beside the Ne'er Pan all your lives, yet know so little about it?" replied the troupe's leader, a wizened old woman whose bright blue eyes missed nothing.

"We needed only to ask permission."

They had been polite about it too. The leader had spoken with great respect and I, in turn, showed them a cache of dry wood for their fire and a game trail that proved fruitful for their dinner.

"Permission," the villagers scoffed. "From a forest?"

"You should listen to the leaves more often. The forest has much knowledge to share with those who have the wit to listen."

The troupe moved on, leaving behind many fond memories and a pox which swept the country-side like wildfire. I do not know what form it took, other than the onset of a fever which I determined from the amount of willow bark being harvested.

Ailiah was like a wraith ghosting through the forest in search of her herbs. Her energy was alarmingly low but she either could not or would not heed my warnings. She was using herself up healing those she could. The villagers took and took, giving nothing in return.

The elder's wife approached Ailiah while she was on the edge of my territory in her never-ending search for the plant that would cure the pox.

"You must come with me now," the elder's wife said. "My daughter is gravely ill and needs your healing touch."

"This illness is very resistant to my small gift, I--"

"You will heal my daughter," the woman said fiercely, "or I will tell the others what you really are."

Ailiah bowed her head in defeat. Neither of them paid attention to the lashing treetops where the leaves

were fairly screaming in anger. Just a few steps closer
to the Ne'er Pan and there might have been a different ending to this story.

The child died and the elder's wife accused Ailiah
of being an abomination. She was locked in a shed as
evidence was collected against her; all her aid and
kindness forgotten. Her great gift was looked upon as
something dark, something sinister.

There was little I could do to help, trapped as I
am within my boundary. But I have an ally in the village. She has aided many gifted men and women over
the years, warning them in time or arranging their
flight. One day, I'm sure, she will join me. This day
she made sure the guards were asleep and set Ailiah
free, urging her to seek the shelter of the Ne'er Pan.

Ailiah had regained some of her strength while
being held prisoner, and was able to outdistance her
pursuers easily. Her route took her along the edge of
the Ne'er Pan, but never quite over the border. When
she put several miles between herself and the village
she slowed and finally found a sheltered spot to rest.

It was so frustrating! She was so close, within a
stone's throw of safety. How could someone whose
own gift was so misunderstood still believe the half-
truths regarding the Ne'er Pan? I strained against my
border but I could not pull free. The leaves moved
without the benefit of the wind as I tried to talk to

her, but she would not hear. It was not my only gift, but it was my only form of communication.

It was the height of irony that she escaped, only to come down with the pox herself. I could have helped her if she would have let me. If she would have crossed over into the Ne'er Pan. She lay on a fallen log when she was too weak to stay upright and continued to ignore the leaves that rustled above her.

The healing mist was just beyond reach. She was deaf to the message of the shivering leaves. My message. The message of the Ne'er Pan.

Golden leaves fell like tears around her as she died.

###

About the Author

Residing in Cobourg, Ontario, Carol was born with a love of reading and writing. She writes a variety of prose: non-fiction, flash fiction, short stories, and novels – in a variety of genres: humour, horror, contemporary, romance, science fiction, and fantasy. She has also explored over 100 different forms of poetry, searching for the perfect verse.

She loves hearing from fans and you can visit Carol on her blog, Random Thoughts of the Writerly Kind - http://randomwriterlythoughts.blogspot.com

Other Short Fiction from Brazen Snake Books

In a Dark Place

At the Water's Edge

The Old Sofa